R0085249324

08/2017

 **W9-DDW-825**

Dear Parent:

Psst . . . you're looking at the Super Secret Weapon of Reading. It's called comics.

STEP INTO READING® COMIC READERS are a perfect step in learning to read. They provide visual cues to the meaning of words and helpfully break out short pieces of dialogue into speech balloons.

Here are some terms commonly associated with comics:
  PANEL: A section of a comic with a box drawn around it.
  CAPTION: Narration that helps set the scene.
  SPEECH BALLOON: A bubble containing dialogue.
  GUTTER: The space between panels.

Tips for reading comics with your child:

- Have your child read the speech balloons while you read the captions.
- Ask your child: What is a character feeling? How can you tell?
- Have your child draw a comic showing what happens after the book is finished.

STEP INTO READING® COMIC READERS are designed to engage and to provide an empowering reading experience. They are also fun. The best-kept secret of comics is that they create lifelong readers. **And that will make you the real hero of the story!**

Jenn — *M. Holm*

Jennifer L. Holm and Matthew Holm
Co-creators of the Babymouse and Squish series

Special thanks to Michelle Cogan, Sarah Lazar, Cindy Ledermann, Dani Light, Tanya Mann, Dan Mokriy, Allison Monterosso, Charnita Belcher, Julia Phelps, Diane Reichenberger, Andrew Tan, David Wiebe, Sharon Woloszyk, and ARC Productions

Published in the United States by Random House Children's Books, a division of Random House LLC, 1745 Broadway, New York, NY 10019, and in Canada by Random House of Canada Limited, Toronto, Penguin Random House Companies.

Step into Reading, Random House, and the Random House colophon are registered trademarks of Random House LLC.

Visit us on the Web!
StepIntoReading.com
randomhouse.com/kids

Educators and librarians, for a variety of teaching tools, visit us at RHTeachersLibrarians.com

ISBN 978-0-385-37310-4 (trade) — ISBN 978-0-375-97194-5 (lib. bdg.) —
ISBN 978-0-375-98185-2 (ebook)
Printed in the United States of America
10 9 8 7 6 5 4 3 2

Barbie
Life in the Dreamhouse

Licensed to Drive

A COMIC READER

Adapted by Mary Tillworth

Based on the screenplay by David Wiebe

Random House 🏠 New York

It is a quiet afternoon
in Barbie's Dreamhouse.

Oh! Mail's here!

Ding-dong!

Crash!

You know, I've had so many careers . . .

It's hard to keep track of all one hundred and thirty-five of them!

And counting!

Ring!
Ring!

Hello?

We heard the squeal.
Did you get it?

Eeeeee!!!

Can you drive me and Teresa to the beach?

The forecast calls for sunny . . .

with a chance of a whole lot of cute guys!

I have my license, but the truth is . . .

I never learned how to drive.

I heard the squeal!

I'll call you later.

Sooo . . . where is it?

You've been waiting a long time for this.

So I wanted to give you something for this special occasion.

Gasp!

It's gorgeous!

Do I mind that Barbie showed me up by putting that car together?

Nope. Doesn't bother me a bit!

Now for a quick check of the mirrors . . .

And we're ready to go.

Screech!!!

Later on . . .

I don't know what I was so worried about.

Ja-jing! Ja-jing!

Ja-jing!

Hi, Barbie!

Clunk!

I'll never learn to drive.

It's that darn *schland poofah*!

To the beach!

Well, I'm still not very good at this whole driving thing. . . .

Twelve-footers have been spotted at Point Doom!

And there are some really big waves, too!

I'm terrified . . .

and loving it!!!

Barbie! Wait!!!

Clunk, clunk, clunk!

What in the world?

Waaaiiit . . .

Thanks for the driving lesson, Ken!

Maybe he can teach me how to drive.

Warning. Objects in the mirror . . .

may be handsomer than they appear.

Vroom!

Screech!